Space Mouse

Richard Saunders
Illustrated by: Phil Gerard Godin

To order additional copies of this book, contact:
Xlibris
1-888-795-4274
www.Xlibris.com
Orders@Xlibris.com

This is the story of Bert Whisperfoot, with middle initial *M*, a most unusual fellow. It all started in my garage late one summer. Like lots of fathers, I have an old car; in my case, it's an eighteen-year-old one called a BMW. I'm an English professor and know nothing about cars, so all I can do is polish mine and drive it on sunny summer days. It makes me feel good because it's big and important looking.

On this particular day, I opened the trunk to get some polishing rags and noticed in one corner what looked like milkweed down, like soft feathers, only from a plant. This was odd since I had cleaned some up just the week before. For a moment, I had thought it was from a fall bouquet that Polly, my wife, had taken to a neighbor. But it couldn't have been because Polly rarely used this car. It had to have been the beginning of a rodent nest, which was not far-fetched. We live in the country where there are lots of field mice who would love a warm spot to camp out for the winter.

As I swept up the milkweed, I was startled by a voice.

"Excuse me," it exclaimed most properly, "did I misstep in moving into this house?"

I looked around. Nope, no one was behind me. I heard a small cough, and looking to the side of the trunk lid, I saw a pair of round black eyes blinking at me. I had never before been spoken to by a mouse. A mouse!

"Was that you?" I asked, leaning toward him.

"Who else would it be?" he replied, as if surprised to be asked. "BMW's the name, short for Bert M. Whisperfoot, at your service."

At first, I was at a loss for words. Could I really be talking to a mouse? Awkwardly, I struggled to make conversation. "Err, err, why the emphasis on the middle initial?" I finally managed. I had no idea mice could talk, much less have names and middle initials. "What does the *M* stand for?"

He responded like a professor answering a student. "Traditionally, all mice have the middle initial *M*. I have no idea when it became a standard practice, but it comes from the recognition that mice are cute and often charming, but potentially mistaken for rats, who are frightening and hated. When you see my middle initial, you know I'm nice." He chuckled, tugging on his vest.

BMW was little, no bigger than your smallest fist, with beautiful gray fur except for his belly, which was perfectly white. His whiskers were long and precisely aligned to either side of his nose like antennas. The slight gray on their tips hinted to me that this was a senior mouse, if such existed. In contrast to his small size, he had a deep voice, not squeaky, and louder than I'd have expected. Unlike most mice in my experience, he wore a dark well-fitted vest, which he frequently tugged down just as I remember my grandfather doing. Additionally, a bright-red headband, a heavy thread actually, encircled his head and ears. He mentioned later that hugging his ears close to his head was necessary because the "noisy world hurts."

BMW

8

The most remarkable thing about BMW was, indeed, his ears. They were almost as large as he was. Imagine an elephant's large ears or ours reaching to the floor. BMW's ears were huge.

Apparently, my guest had assumed that the BMW insignia on my old car was actually a welcoming sign with his initials. "Seeing that I'm a famous mouse and all." He thought I would have recognized him because, recently, our president had honored him at a retirement party from the NASA space program. I had to confess that I wasn't aware of his importance.

At this point, he seemed hesitant to talk further about himself, and I didn't press him. I wanted to make him feel secure in my trunk, hoping he wouldn't leave. I wanted to hear more from this space mouse. Why would he be important to the space program?

Much to BMW's horror, our old cat, Gordon, just then chose to visit the garage and rub against my leg. I doubt that very old cat could ever catch a mouse. I was not certain he even saw my unusual visitor. Nevertheless, BMW was gone in a shot. And I was left scolding the perplexed cat. I was fearful that I'd never hear the story I'm about to relate.

BMW didn't return that day or the next. I didn't tell my family about BMW. Most certainly, they would have thought me crazy: a talking mouse, the space program, a presidential citation . . . come on.

To my relief, a few days later, I found my mouse friend sitting atop the car as if nothing had happened.

"Sorry, I left you so abruptly," he began. "Us mice have an automatic scram alert with cats, no matter how old, slow, and harmless. I really should have known better."

BMW's brief encounter with Gordon the cat didn't end there. That clever mouse recognized something I hadn't. His bold confidence, common to astronauts, was nothing Gordon had ever seen in a mouse. The huge ears, cocky indifference, and that vest so confused my cat that over time, he and BMW actually became comfortable with each other. Soon after their first encounter, there was that little mouse combing Gordon's tail. Even more charming was the old cat gently carrying BMW, like a kitten, by the scruff of the neck to the top of a garden post for one of our conversations.

Over the next several weeks, BMW settled into his house of the same name. I was intrigued with the little fellow. Each day, I couldn't wait to check the car trunk. Sure enough, he was usually there.

"Good morning, my good friend," he'd say. I wished my children were so polite.

As the summer passed into fall, BMW's nest got bigger and bigger, and we were close friends. But he still didn't volunteer much more about himself. Often, as I polished my old car, he would sit on the hood, washing his ears—no small task, I might add. We'd make small talk about the weather, the car, or how I had to be careful not to slam the doors or trunk. "It hurts my ears!" he said. Nevertheless, I sensed that he liked my company and was used to being with human beings.

As far as I could tell, BMW had no mouse friends. I was becoming concerned that he was lonely. It is often said that if you see one mouse, there are bound to be many others nearby, but this didn't seem to be the case. I had to believe this was because he was different. He was a mouse with huge ears who could talk.

One day, I had an idea. I brought BMW a piece of cheese. As I expected, he was absolutely delighted.

"Gorgonzola, my favorite," he exclaimed, washing his hands in a mouse-like fashion before touching the cheese. His front paws moved, one then the other, before his face so rapidly you could hardly see that each paw was being carefully licked. Then like a kid offered candy, he grabbed the piece of cheese in both paws and nibbled it away as fast as he had washed his hands.

Then as I had hoped, his ecstasy with the smelly gift made him talkative in appreciation. Smacking his lips, he leaned back in his cozy nest and said, "I've decided to write my autobiography. I know you're an English professor. I wonder if you would help me."

I answered as indifferently as I could manage, "I'd be pleased to help. Why don't I just take your dictation, and we can polish it up later. I've paper and pencil right here in the car. I'm ready. Go ahead."

And just like that, he began.

"I was born in China, near the South China Sea, in the Guangdong Province. It's a fairly well-known place. It used to be called Canton. It has over a hundred million people. Even though I was thought to be very smart by my teachers, I was teased by the other mouse kids who laughed at my big ears. They would torment me by squeaking loudly 'cause they knew it hurt. My mother and father, who didn't have big ears, loved me anyway, and someday, they assured me, I'd be respected and appreciated in spite of my ears, provided, of course, that I worked hard in school.

"My mother used this red silk cord to tie back my ears so that loud noises would be less painful. The cord was a family treasure said to have been snatched from the Chinese emperor's robe by one of my naughtier relatives a hundred years ago. It didn't help the teasing, but I cherished it. Those kids were just jealous. None of them had such a beautiful string, and they knew of the legend of how it came into my family. Their teasing was envy.

"Studying was my escape. I actually learned to understand and then speak English by visiting tourist spots and universities. My province has dozens of 'em. I would sit inside the lampshades in restaurants without being noticed . . . most of the time. Big college lecture halls, packed with rows of chairs, made a small guy like me invisible.

"I remember my first conversation with a visiting American speaker at the Guangdong Institute of Technology. I had hidden inside the speaker's podium, and when he finished, I asked a question without thinking. My voice was picked up by the podium microphone and boomed out into the hall. The speaker, not knowing where the question came from, answered it casually. Only when I hopped up on the podium to thank him did he realize that he had responded to a mouse!

"That was the beginning of my American experience. Later, some visiting lecturers from the American Space Exploration Center actually asked for me. They were interested in my ears and hearing, and especially that I spoke English. I had become a university curiosity. My folks were worried that this interest was not, necessarily, in my best interests. They'd heard of what happened to mice in laboratories. But one scientist convinced them that the American space program offered a unique opportunity for their son."

BMW smoothed back his ears with both paws like a teenager with long hair, pulled up a corner of one of my polishing rags, flicked off a wisp of lint from his tail, and said, "Now here's the exciting part.

"Those American scientists did some hearing tests. I liked their attention, having been laughed at for so long. It turned out that I could hear better than even I had realized. They had a secret project tailored just for me." He furrowed his brow with pretended self-importance. "I came to America nearly ten years ago, in their words, to add a unique dimension to the science of space travel using my ears.

"I wasn't to be kept in a cage or owned by anyone. My only commitment was to be part of the secret space program. When not working, I was on my own. I got here to your farm by myself. It's simple. I stowed away in a lady's big handbag, unbeknownst to the owner. As you know, handbags can be very large and are rarely zipped closed. My travel plans are always flexible. The important detail is selecting the bag of a lady headed to the airport.

"I stay in the bag until arrival at the passenger screening line where things can get a bit challenging, but not for me. Since my skeleton would show under the handbag x-ray screener, as the bag enters it, I jump out and away from the bag. The officials frequently see my mouse skeleton on their screen, but since it doesn't appear among the bag's contents, they never suspect a handbag stowaway. They'd rather assume a mouse is somewhere in their machine. As the bag moves out of the screener, I simply leap back in to continue my trip. The ultimate trick is to avoid being discovered by the handbag owner as they fish into it for something. You can imagine how upsetting that could be.

"Now back to my story. For years, even before space exploration, mice and, yes, people too have wondered about intelligent life existing on other planets. Of the millions of planets out there in space, in our solar system and others, it does seem unlikely that our Earth is the only one with life, doesn't it?"

He stopped talking for a moment, stood up, and stretched. One ear had slipped from under his headband. He repositioned it automatically and then said, "Let's go for a walk, and I'll show you something."

I must admit I couldn't imagine what this had to do with his autobiography.

We live on a hill overlooking a small college.

"Actually, I decided to look for a retirement place here because of that school," he allowed, slightly out of breath as he hurried before me along the path to our high meadow. I marveled that here, I was chatting with a mouse who was leading me, a human being, on a walk to explain something about space exploration! How would I ever explain this to my family?

24

"See that building just beyond the tall chimney?" he asked as we looked down the valley to the north. I nodded, and he went on. "That's the heating plant, and the men are talking with their boss about the night shift."

I assumed that this was only a presumption since the heating plant, though visible from our hilltop, was six miles away.

Smiling, he went on, "Listen hard. Can you hear them? I can."

I didn't doubt BMW for a minute. The little mouse's hearing was extraordinary.

"Okay, let's get back to the dictation," he said as we walked back toward the house. "This is what those space scientists had in mind.

"About fifteen years ago, three planets like our Earth were discovered far, far away in space. It was so far away that to travel there would take many years in a rocket faster than any rocket ever made. Clearly, visiting these planets to see if people were there was not possible. So the alternative was to attempt to hear voices from them deep in space.

"Look up the SETI project. It's about space listening. Google it. I was on the ground floor of it. Me, a mouse! Anyway, that SETI project involved big antennas directed at outer space. But in the midst of Earth's noise, nothing yet has been picked up. That's where I came in!

"The scientists asked me to ride in a satellite. With my keen hearing, away from Earth's noise, I was to listen for any possible space messages.

"I thought it would be neat. I had a special mouse-size space suit and a leash for control. Remember, there's no gravity up there. My helmet was real cool, considering my big ears. The astronauts were amused. I was like a big bug floating among them.

"You'll hear that space is pretty quiet, but it isn't for a guy with my hearing. The world beneath from space is beautiful, but more than that, it's the sounds. I heard stuff like the rumble of elephant herds on the African savanna, the swooshing wings of big bird migrations, and the crunchings of giant icebergs—sounds that most people will never experience. It's a world orchestra that only I could appreciate from space."

The next morning, as I entered the garage, BMW scurried up to a shelf and jumped onto the roof of my car, saying breathlessly, "Just had a run. Gotta stay in shape, you know. Ready for dictation?

"Remember that my role in the space program was to listen for any soft signals from outer space, not Earth. We had special time periods for this when the satellite was farthest from Earth. All noise in the capsule was eliminated as much as possible—no music, no talk, no fans, no machinery, nothing. Nevertheless, I never did hear anything from outer space, but sounds from Earth were always there, often muffled or garbled like the sounds from a football stadium in the fall. The space capsule was still too noisy for me to hear anything meaningful from space, so I guess you'd have to say the project was not a success."

"But you got a presidential citation," I said.

"Just let me finish. What I did hear was terribly important. Actually, I'm not supposed to talk about it. I'll have to figure a way so that it can be included in my autobiography. Let me think about it for a while."

So for the time being, the autobiography dictation was on hold. The relationship with my furry friend continued as a secret just between the two of us.

One warm fall day, Mr. Mouse, I called him that sometimes, and I were just sitting together—he, hanging out of my shirt pocket and me, lounging on the warm ground. I was commenting on the cloud formations so beautifully viewed from that high meadow.

He said, "You can see the moon and the sun at the same time today. That's neat."

I added, "We speak of the man in the moon because if you look closely, you can imagine an outline of a face."

He answered, "In China, we see it differently, and imagine a rabbit calling it a hare in the moon." He continued talking as if I had asked a question, which I hadn't. "Actually, the reason I received the president's commendation wasn't related to the space listening project at all. It was something that happened unexpectedly while the space team and I were in the satellite."

"Oh?" I answered casually.

With a subtle excitement in his unusual voice, he went on as if I wasn't there. His ears were laid back and his eyes wide. "The scientists on the satellite were making small talk when one jokingly asked me if I had overheard any bad guys down there, pointing toward Earth. And just then I, indeed, heard something. Our space capsule was passing over the Atlantic Ocean."

His tail whipped once above his head. The hair on his neck stood up. His ears were now fully upright, having slipped from under his headband. He was really getting into his story. "I was lying on my stomach in my hammock with my ears toward Earth. That day, Earth voices were loud and clear from a ship alone on the Atlantic Ocean."

I interrupted, "Didn't you hear humans speaking all the time?"

"Yes, but these weren't humans. They were mice. That's why I noticed. They were frightened, talking about having to 'get off this boat.'"

"You were hearing mice," I said.

"Of course, I am a mouse, remember? Obviously, they were stowaways. Mice on ships always are. We're pretty good travelers, generally, and it's free, with plenty of food and comfort, except in airplanes. Mice usually set up quarters in the ship's galley [kitchen] or behind the cabinets or stove where it's warm and well supplied.

"Those mice had overheard the crew being told that, on command, they were to abandon ship. The word used was *abandon*, meaning 'jump off the boat before it docked'–not a routine command. This was what got the attention of the mice *and* me. Then there was something about a 'big bomb.' As soon as I heard *bomb*, I yelled what I was hearing to my astronaut colleagues. It had to be reported, but would the word of a mouse, hearing mice, be just laughed off by the FBI?

"It was decided that I'd talk with the agents by phone without telling them that I was a mouse. My deep voice came in handy, I can tell you."

I interrupted, "You mean that was you?" I remembered that some time ago, a ship was stopped near New York Harbor by the coast guard, and the crew was arrested. A bomb was found on board, and it was defused safely. No other details were reported.

BMW answered proudly, "Yup, and for that, the president gave me a medal and a retirement party."

+++++

So that was BMW's story recounted to you, dear reader, for the first time.

I had sometimes wondered if one day, my mouse friend would disappear. I imagined how I'd anguish: did an animal kill him? Did he get sick and crawl away to die? And stuff like that. One's imagination can do awful things. Fortunately, BMW was more thoughtful than that. There he was on the same garden post where we'd chatted so many times. Almost eye to eye with me, he sat adjusting those big ears and the red emperor's headband cord.

"You and Gordon have been my only friends since I left the space center," he began solemnly. "I've not met another giant-eared mouse in America, and other common mice simply laugh at me. I'm not married and have no children. It's a very sad acknowledgment for a mouse as we usually have very big families. So I have decided to return to China to find a big-eared lady friend."I was saddened, but I couldn't argue with him. I completely understood. I even offered to take him to the airport in an old tote bag.

Bag Claim 5-10

Ground Transport

Parking

40

Just as the autumn leaves began to fall, BMW left me at the waiting area for international departures at Boston's Logan Airport. I had dutifully set my mouse-occupied tote bag next to the very large handbag of a pretty young Asian lady. My last image of BMW was his waving paw as he quickly disappeared into that bag. I stayed long enough to see the lady walking onto the departure ramp as the sign next to the boarding gate flashed Hong Kong, China.

I often think of my old friend and wonder if he really found happiness in China. I check out the trunk of my old car by habit. I still polish the chrome and take short drives, and I never, ever slam the door . . . because you never know.

The End

Printed in the United States
By Bookmasters